Tales from Trinidad & Tobago: Exploring Folklore and Legends

Contents

Papa Bois: Guardian of the Forests 3
The Dance of the Moko Jumbies: A Tale of Unity and Harmony 7
The Soucouyant's Secret: A Tale of Courage and Protection 10
The Temptation of La Diablesse: A Tale of Love and Loss 13
The Legacy of King Lopinot: A Tale of Courage and Resilience..15
The Song of the Mermaid: A Tale of Love and Redemption...17
The Sacred Guardians: A Tale of Respect and Redemption...20
The Rhythms of Unity: The Legend of Bongo Man 22
Echoes of the Past: Unraveling the Mystery of Devil's Woodyard 24
The Sanctum of Serenity: The Legend of Mount Saint Benedict 26

Papa Bois: Guardian of the Forests

In the heart of Trinidad's lush forests, where the emerald canopy stretches endlessly and the air hums with the symphony of nature, there dwells a legendary figure known as Papa Bois. He is the guardian of the wildlife, the protector of the natural world that thrives within the verdant embrace of the trees. Papa Bois is a figure of awe and reverence, his presence whispered about in tales passed down through generations.

According to folklore, Papa Bois is a majestic being, appearing as a tall, muscular man with the legs of a goat and the antlers of a deer. His eyes gleam with ancient wisdom, and his presence commands respect. It is said that he roams the forests at night, unseen by most, ensuring the safety of animals and punishing those who dare to harm them.

One moonlit night, a group of hunters ventured into the depths of the forest, their minds consumed by the thrill of the chase and the promise of a bountiful catch. Ignoring the warnings of elders who spoke of Papa Bois and the consequences of disrespecting the creatures of the land, they pushed deeper into the wilderness, their laughter echoing through the trees.

As they ventured further into the forest, the air grew thick with tension, and the sounds of the night took on an otherworldly quality. Strange sights flickered at the edge of their vision, and eerie sounds echoed through the darkness. Still, the hunters pressed on, fueled by their desire for conquest and oblivious to the consequences of their actions.

Suddenly, as if materializing from the shadows themselves, Papa Bois appeared before them. His presence was awe-inspiring, his eyes piercing through the darkness with a steely gaze. The hunters froze in their tracks, their bravado evaporating in an instant as they beheld the legendary figure before them.

With a voice like thunder, Papa Bois spoke, his words resonating through the forest. He recounted tales of the land's rich history, of the creatures that called it home, and of the sacred bond between man and nature. He spoke of the importance of respecting all living beings and living in harmony with the natural world.

As Papa Bois spoke, the hunters listened in rapt attention, their hearts heavy with remorse for their actions. They realized the folly of their ways, the arrogance that had driven them to disregard the warnings of their elders and the sanctity of the land. In that moment, they understood the true meaning of respect and the interconnectedness of all life.

With a solemn nod, Papa Bois vanished into the night, leaving the hunters to ponder the lessons they had learned. From that day forward, they vowed to honor the natural world and to tread lightly upon the earth, mindful of the creatures that called it home.

As the hunters made their way out of the forest, they found themselves guided by a newfound sense of reverence for the land and its inhabitants. The once familiar path seemed to take on a new light, each tree and each blade of grass imbued with a sense of sacredness.

Word of their encounter with Papa Bois spread quickly through the village, becoming a cautionary tale passed down through generations. The legend of Papa Bois lived on, a timeless reminder of the importance of respecting nature and all its inhabitants.

Meanwhile, deep within the heart of the forest, Papa Bois continued his eternal vigil, watching over the land and its creatures with unwavering devotion. His presence was felt in every rustle of leaves and every whisper of the wind, a silent guardian standing watch over the natural world.

As the seasons turned and the years passed, Papa Bois remained a figure of mystery and reverence, his legend woven into the fabric of Trinidad's rich tapestry of folklore. For those who dared to venture into the wilderness, let the tale of Papa Bois serve as a reminder of the importance of respecting nature and all its inhabitants.

In the years that followed, the hunters who had encountered Papa Bois became stewards of the land, working tirelessly to protect the forests and the creatures that called them home. They formed alliances with the indigenous peoples who had long revered Papa Bois as a guardian spirit, learning from them the ancient wisdom of living in harmony with nature.

Together, they embarked on a mission to preserve Trinidad's natural heritage, establishing protected areas and conservation initiatives to safeguard the forests for future generations. Their efforts bore fruit, and over time, the forests flourished once more, teeming with life and vitality.

But Papa Bois was not only a guardian of the forests; he was also a symbol of resilience and hope in the face of adversity. In times of hardship and strife, the people of Trinidad looked to Papa Bois for guidance and inspiration, drawing strength from his unwavering commitment to protecting the natural world.

And so, the legend of Papa Bois lived on, a beacon of light in a world filled with darkness, reminding all who encountered him of the importance of respecting nature and all its inhabitants. For Papa Bois was more than just a myth; he was a living embodiment of the sacred bond between man and the natural world.

As the years turned into decades and the decades turned into centuries, the legend of Papa Bois continued to resonate with the people of Trinidad, inspiring future generations to embrace a life of harmony and respect for the land. His legacy lived on in the hearts and minds of all who heard his tale, a timeless reminder of the interconnectedness of all life on Earth.

And so, let us remember the legend of Papa Bois, the guardian of the forests, the protector of the wildlife, and the eternal symbol of the sacred bond between man and nature. For in his story, we find the true essence of what it means to live in harmony with the natural world, respecting all living beings and treading lightly upon the Earth.

In the lush forests of Trinidad, where the emerald canopy stretches endlessly and the air hums with the symphony of nature, Papa Bois watches over the land with unwavering devotion. His presence is felt in every rustle of leaves and every whisper of the wind, a silent guardian standing watch over the natural world.

And though the years may pass, and the world may change, the legend of Papa Bois will endure, a timeless reminder of the importance of respecting nature and all its inhabitants. For in his story, we find the true essence of what it means to live in harmony with the natural world, embracing a life of reverence and respect for the land.

The Dance of the Moko Jumbies: A Tale of Unity and Harmony

In the vibrant land of Trinidad, where the rhythms of life pulse through every street and alley, there exists a magical tradition steeped in folklore and legend. It is the tradition of the Moko Jumbies, towering stilt walkers adorned in vibrant costumes, who dance with grace and elegance, captivating the hearts of all who witness their spectacle.

Legend has it that the Moko Jumbies possess mystical abilities, able to ward off evil spirits and bring blessings to communities. Their towering presence symbolizes strength and resilience, standing tall as guardians of the land and its people.

During a time of great strife and conflict, when the land was torn apart by division and discord, a group of Moko Jumbies emerged to bring peace and harmony to the land. With their towering stature and graceful movements, they traversed the streets of Trinidad, their rhythmic beats echoing through the air like a heartbeat of unity.

As they danced, their vibrant costumes swirled around them like a kaleidoscope of colors, mesmerizing all who witnessed their spectacle. People from all walks of life gathered in awe, drawn together by the power of the Moko Jumbies' dance.

With each step, the Moko Jumbies weaved a tapestry of harmony and unity, their movements telling a story of resilience and cultural heritage. They danced with grace and elegance, their stilted strides defying gravity as they soared above the crowd.

As the sun dipped below the horizon and the stars twinkled in the night sky, the Moko Jumbies' dance reached its crescendo. Their rhythmic beats reverberated through the land, driving away the shadows of fear and discord, and filling the hearts of all who witnessed their spectacle with hope and joy.

In that moment, the people of Trinidad were united as one, their differences fading away in the glow of the Moko Jumbies' dance. They danced together in the streets, their laughter ringing out like a chorus of angels, as they celebrated the power of unity and cultural heritage.

The Moko Jumbies danced on, their graceful movements transcending time and space, as they continued to weave their magic across the land. With each step, they brought blessings to the communities they passed through, leaving behind a trail of peace and harmony in their wake.

And so, the legend of the Moko Jumbies' dance lived on, passed down through generations as a testament to the power of unity and cultural heritage. In times of strife and conflict, the people of Trinidad would gather together, drawing strength from the memory of the Moko Jumbies' dance, and finding solace in the knowledge that unity and harmony were always within their reach.

As the years passed, the Moko Jumbies continued to dance across the land, their graceful movements a symbol of resilience and hope for all who witnessed their spectacle. And though the world may change and time may march on, the spirit of the Moko Jumbies' dance will endure, a timeless reminder of the power of unity and cultural heritage.

In the heart of Trinidad, where the rhythms of life pulse through every street and alley, the Moko Jumbies continue to dance, their vibrant costumes swirling around them like a kaleidoscope of colors. With each step, they bring blessings to the land and its people, their graceful movements weaving a tapestry of harmony and unity.

And so, let us remember the legend of the Moko Jumbies' dance, and the power it holds to bring peace and harmony to the land. For in their graceful movements and rhythmic beats, we find the true essence of Trinidadian folklore, a celebration of unity and cultural heritage that transcends time and space.

In the years that followed, the legend of the Moko Jumbies' dance continued to inspire the people of Trinidad, reminding them of the importance of unity and cultural heritage in times of strife and conflict. The Moko Jumbies' dance became a symbol of resilience and hope, a beacon of light in a world filled with darkness.

And so, the people of Trinidad gathered together, drawn by the memory of the Moko Jumbies' dance, and found strength in their unity. They danced together in the streets, their laughter ringing out like a chorus of angels, as they celebrated the power of cultural heritage to bring peace and harmony to the land.

As the years passed, the legend of the Moko Jumbies' dance lived on, passed down through generations as a testament to the enduring power of unity and cultural heritage. And though the world may change and time may march on, the spirit of the Moko Jumbies' dance will endure, a timeless reminder of the importance of coming together as one people, united in our diversity and our shared humanity.

And so, let us remember the legend of the Moko Jumbies' dance, and the power it holds to bring peace and harmony to the land. For in their graceful movements and rhythmic beats, we find the true essence of Trinidadian folklore, a celebration of unity and cultural heritage that transcends time and space.

In the heart of Trinidad, where the rhythms of life pulse through every street and alley, the Moko Jumbies continue to dance, their vibrant costumes swirling around them like a kaleidoscope of colors. With each step, they bring blessings to the land and its people, their graceful movements weaving a tapestry of harmony and unity.

And so, let us remember the legend of the Moko Jumbies' dance, and the power it holds to bring peace and harmony to the land. For in their graceful movements and rhythmic beats, we find the true essence of Trinidadian folklore, a celebration of unity and cultural heritage that transcends time and space.

The Soucouyant's Secret: A Tale of Courage and Protection

In the heart of Tobago, where the lush greenery meets the azure waters of the Caribbean Sea, lies a village shrouded in whispers and superstitions. Deep within its confines, hidden from the prying eyes of outsiders, dwells a malevolent spirit known as the Soucouyant. This fearsome creature, said to take the form of an old woman by day and transform into a fiery ball of energy by night, strikes fear into the hearts of all who hear her name.

Legend has it that the Soucouyant preys on unsuspecting victims, feeding on their blood and leaving behind a trail of destruction in her wake. Her fiery presence illuminates the night sky, casting a sinister glow over the village as she seeks out her next victim. For generations, the villagers have lived in fear of the Soucouyant's wrath, their homes barricaded against her malevolent presence.

However, amidst the fear and superstition, there exists a secret known to only a few brave souls - the secret to defeating the Soucouyant. It is said that a brave young man, armed with courage and determination, discovered the key to warding off the evil spirit. By sprinkling salt along doorways and windowsills, he created a barrier that prevented the Soucouyant from entering homes, effectively protecting the villagers from her wrath.

With this newfound knowledge, the villagers banded together, determined to protect their community from the Soucouyant's malevolent presence. Armed with sacks of salt and steely resolve, they worked tirelessly to fortify their homes, creating a barrier that would keep the evil spirit at bay. Their efforts were not in vain, for as night fell and the Soucouyant's fiery form descended upon the village, she found herself thwarted by the protective barrier of salt.

Enraged by her inability to enter the homes of the villagers, the Soucouyant unleashed her fury upon the village, her fiery form casting shadows of terror across the land. But the villagers stood firm, their resolve unshaken as they faced the malevolent spirit head-on. With each passing moment, the Soucouyant's powers waned, her fiery form flickering like a dying ember until she vanished into the darkness, defeated by the courage and determination of the villagers.

As dawn broke and the first light of morning illuminated the village, the villagers emerged from their homes, victorious in their battle against the Soucouyant. Their homes stood untouched, their families safe from harm, thanks to the protective barrier of salt that had kept the evil spirit at bay. And though the memory of the Soucouyant's wrath lingered in the air, the villagers found solace in the knowledge that they had triumphed over darkness and fear.

From that day forward, the legend of the Soucouyant's secret spread throughout the village, becoming a tale of courage and protection passed down through generations. The villagers continued to fortify their homes with salt, ensuring that they remained safe from the malevolent spirit's wrath. And though the Soucouyant may have been defeated, her legend lived on, a reminder of the power of courage and unity in the face of darkness.

As the years passed and the village prospered, the memory of the Soucouyant faded into legend, becoming little more than a whispered tale told to frighten children into obedience. But for those who had witnessed the bravery of the villagers in the face of the evil spirit's wrath, the legend of the Soucouyant's secret remained a testament to the power of courage and determination in the face of adversity.

And so, let us remember the tale of the Soucouyant's secret, and the courage of the villagers who stood firm against the malevolent spirit's wrath. For in their bravery and determination, we find the true essence of Tobagonian folklore, a celebration of resilience and unity in the face of darkness and fear.

In the heart of Tobago, where the lush greenery meets the azure waters of the Caribbean Sea, lies a village shrouded in whispers and superstitions. Deep within its confines, hidden from the prying eyes of outsiders, dwells the legend of the Soucouyant's secret - a tale of courage and protection that continues to inspire generations to come.

The Temptation of La Diablesse: A Tale of Love and Loss

In the heart of Trinidadian folklore, amidst the vibrant colors of carnival and the rhythms of calypso, lies a tale of seduction and mystery. It is the legend of La Diablesse, a bewitching woman who haunts the depths of the forest, her beauty as enchanting as it is dangerous. Legend has it that she appears at night, dressed in a long flowing gown and a wide-brimmed hat that conceals her face, her presence casting a spell of temptation upon all who encounter her.

Those who come across La Diablesse are drawn in by her allure, unable to resist her charms. Their hearts beat with longing as they follow her into the depths of the forest, their footsteps guided by the promise of forbidden pleasure. But behind her beguiling facade lies a darkness that few can comprehend, for those who succumb to her temptations are said to suffer a terrible fate, never to be seen again.

Among the villagers, tales abound of men who have fallen under La Diablesse's spell, their lives forever altered by the allure of her beauty. They speak in hushed tones of lost loves and broken hearts, of dreams shattered and souls consumed by desire. Yet amidst the tragedy, there are whispers of hope - for only those with pure hearts and strong wills can resist La Diablesse's advances and escape her grasp.

It is said that La Diablesse preys upon the vulnerable, those whose hearts are filled with longing and whose minds are clouded by desire. She appears to them in their darkest moments, offering a glimpse of paradise amidst the shadows of the forest. But behind her seductive smile lies a hunger that cannot be sated, a thirst for souls that drives her ever onwards in her quest for companionship.

And so it was that one fateful night, amidst the whispers of the forest and the soft glow of the moon, a young man named Miguel found himself ensnared by La Diablesse's spell. His heart ached with longing as he gazed upon her beauty, his footsteps guided by the promise of forbidden pleasure. But deep within his soul, a flicker of resistance burned bright, a spark of hope that whispered of salvation amidst the darkness.

As Miguel followed La Diablesse into the depths of the forest, his heart pounded with fear and anticipation. He knew the dangers that lay ahead, the temptations that awaited him amidst the shadows. But with each step, he drew strength from the memory of his true love, a beacon of light amidst the darkness that threatened to consume him.

As they ventured deeper into the forest, La Diablesse's allure grew stronger, her beauty shining like a beacon amidst the shadows. But Miguel remained steadfast in his resolve, his heart filled with love for the woman he had left behind. With each passing moment, he felt the grip of temptation loosen its hold, his footsteps guided by the purity of his heart and the strength of his will.

And so it was that as they reached the heart of the forest, La Diablesse's spell was broken, her beauty fading into the shadows as Miguel's true love shone brightly in his heart. With a final cry of despair, La Diablesse vanished into the darkness, her seductive smile replaced by the memory of a love that could not be broken.

As Miguel emerged from the depths of the forest, his heart filled with gratitude for the strength that had carried him through the darkness. He returned to his village a changed man, his spirit tempered by the trials he had faced and the love that had guided him through the shadows. And though the memory of

La Diablesse's temptation lingered in the air, Miguel knew that he had emerged victorious, his heart forever free from the darkness that had threatened to consume him.

And so, let us remember the tale of La Diablesse's temptation, and the strength of the human spirit in the face of darkness and desire. For in Miguel's triumph over temptation, we find the true essence of Trinidadian folklore, a celebration of love and resilience amidst the shadows of the forest. And though the legend of La Diablesse may live on in whispers and tales, let us remember that it is the purity of the heart and the strength of the will that will ultimately guide us through the darkness and into the light.

The Legacy of King Lopinot: A Tale of Courage and Resilience

In the rugged mountainous region of Trinidad, nestled amidst the verdant greenery, lies the village of Lopinot. Named after a legendary figure known as King Lopinot, this village is steeped in history and folklore, with tales of bravery and resilience echoing through the ages. According to legend, King Lopinot was a fierce warrior and leader who defended his people against invaders with unmatched courage and cunning.

King Lopinot's story begins centuries ago, in a time when Trinidad was a land of untamed wilderness and tribal warfare. Born into a noble family, Lopinot was destined for greatness from a young age. His strength and leadership skills were evident even in his youth, and as he grew older, he became a formidable warrior, leading his people into battle against their enemies.

With each victory, King Lopinot's legend grew, his name whispered in awe and reverence by those who witnessed his bravery on the battlefield. He was known for his unwavering courage and his strategic brilliance, outsmarting his foes at every turn and leading his people to victory time and time again.

But King Lopinot's greatest triumph came when he faced off against a formidable enemy, a rival tribe that sought to conquer his lands and subjugate his people. With his back against the wall and his people's future hanging in the balance, King Lopinot rose to the challenge, rallying his warriors and devising a daring plan to thwart the invaders.

The battle that followed was fierce and bloody, with both sides fighting tooth and nail for victory. But in the end, it was King Lopinot's cunning and leadership that carried the day, as he outmaneuvered his enemies and emerged victorious against all odds. The invaders were routed, their forces scattered, and King Lopinot's people were saved from certain doom.

In the aftermath of the battle, King Lopinot's legend only grew, as tales of his bravery and cunning spread far and wide. He became a symbol of hope and resilience for his people, a beacon of light in a dark and tumultuous time. And though he eventually passed into legend, his legacy lived on, inspiring future generations to honor his memory and preserve their cultural heritage.

Today, the ruins of King Lopinot's fortress still stand as a testament to his greatness, a silent reminder of the courage and resilience that defined his life. Locals gather at the site to pay homage to their legendary hero, honoring his memory with songs and stories passed down through generations.

But King Lopinot's legacy goes beyond mere monuments and relics. His spirit lives on in the hearts and minds of the people of Lopinot, inspiring them to carry on his legacy of courage and resilience in the face of adversity. They draw strength from his example, knowing that as long as they remember his story, they will never be defeated.

And so, the story of King Lopinot continues to echo through the ages, a tale of courage and resilience that transcends time and space. His legend lives on in the hearts of all who hear it, a reminder of the power of bravery and determination in the face of impossible odds.

In the mountainous region of Trinidad, amidst the rugged terrain and lush greenery, the village of Lopinot stands as a living testament to the legacy of its legendary hero. And though centuries may pass and the world may change, the spirit of King Lopinot will forever endure, a beacon of hope and inspiration for all who seek to follow in his footsteps.

The Song of the Mermaid: A Tale of Love and Redemption

Maracas Bay, with its pristine golden sands and crystal-clear turquoise waters, has long been a place of wonder and beauty. But hidden beneath the waves lies a secret known only to a few: the existence of the Mermaid of Maracas. According to legend, she is a beautiful maiden with long flowing hair and shimmering scales, who emerges from the depths of the ocean to sing to sailors and fishermen.

The legend of the Mermaid of Maracas has been passed down through generations, whispered in hushed tones by those who have caught glimpses of her ethereal beauty. It is said that her enchanting voice has the power to calm storms and guide lost ships to safety, earning her the reverence and respect of all who sail the waters of Maracas Bay.

But the mermaid's magic is not to be trifled with, for those who dare to capture her or reveal her secrets are met with misfortune. Many have tried to capture her beauty, lured by the promise of wealth and fame, only to meet a tragic end. And so, the mermaid remains a mysterious and elusive figure, her presence felt but her secrets closely guarded.

Among the villagers of Maracas Bay, tales of the mermaid are spoken of in reverent tones, a reminder of the power and beauty of the ocean that surrounds them. But for one young fisherman named Diego, the legend of the Mermaid of Maracas held a special fascination. From a young age, he had been drawn to the sea, captivated by its mysteries and its wonders.

As Diego grew older, he spent more and more time on the water, honing his skills as a fisherman and learning the ways of the ocean. He had heard the tales of the Mermaid of Maracas, and though he had never seen her with his own eyes, he felt a deep connection to the mysterious creature who inhabited the waters of his home.

One fateful night, as Diego sailed the waters of Maracas Bay, he heard a hauntingly beautiful melody drifting on the breeze. Intrigued, he followed the sound, his heart pounding with excitement as he drew closer to the source of the music. And then, emerging from the depths of the ocean, he saw her: the Mermaid of Maracas, her long flowing hair cascading over her shimmering scales as she sang her enchanting song.

Mesmerized by her beauty and captivated by her song, Diego felt a sense of wonder wash over him as he gazed upon the mermaid. Her voice was like nothing he had ever heard before, filling him with a sense of peace and tranquility that he had never known. In that moment, he knew that he had found something truly special, something that would change his life forever.

For days, Diego returned to the waters of Maracas Bay, drawn by the siren song of the mermaid and the beauty of her presence. He spent hours listening to her sing, losing himself in the magic of her voice and the mysteries of the ocean. And with each passing day, he felt himself falling more deeply in love with the mermaid, her enchanting presence filling his heart with joy and wonder.

But as Diego's love for the mermaid grew stronger, so too did his desire to share her beauty with the world. He began to dream of capturing her image and revealing her secrets to the world, blinded by the promise of fame and fortune that awaited him. And though he knew the dangers that lay ahead, he could not resist the temptation to possess the mermaid's beauty for himself.

And so it was that one fateful night, Diego set out to capture the mermaid, driven by his desire to possess her beauty and reveal her secrets to the world. But as he reached out to touch her shimmering scales, the mermaid's enchanting song turned to a mournful lament, and with a cry of anguish, she vanished beneath the waves, leaving Diego alone and filled with regret.

In the days that followed, Diego searched the waters of Maracas Bay for any sign of the mermaid, but she was gone, her presence nothing more than a memory. And though he had lost her forever, Diego knew that he had learned a valuable lesson: that some beauty is meant to be cherished from afar, and that the mysteries of the ocean are not ours to possess, but to admire and respect from a distance. And so, he returned to the waters of Maracas Bay, humbled by his experience, and filled with a newfound appreciation for the wonders of the sea.

The Sacred Guardians: A Tale of Respect and Redemption

In the heart of Trinidadian folklore, amidst the lush greenery of the island's landscape, stands the majestic Silk Cotton Tree. Revered as a sacred symbol of strength and resilience, these towering giants are believed to be inhabited by spirits that protect the land and its inhabitants. But there is also a darker side to the Silk Cotton Tree, as it is said to be cursed by those who disrespect its sacredness.

The legend of the curse of the Silk Cotton Tree is whispered in hushed tones among the villagers, a cautionary tale passed down through generations. Tales abound of individuals who dared to harm or cut down these sacred trees, only to suffer mysterious accidents or misfortunes soon after. It serves as a solemn reminder of the importance of respecting nature and the spirits that dwell within it.

Among the villagers, there is a deep reverence for the Silk Cotton Tree, with rituals and ceremonies held to honor its sacredness. Offerings of fruits and flowers are placed at the base of the trees, and prayers are whispered to the spirits that dwell within their branches. For the villagers understand the importance of maintaining a harmonious relationship with the natural world, and they know that to disrespect the Silk Cotton Tree is to invite the wrath of the spirits that protect it.

But despite the warnings and admonitions, there are those who dare to defy the sacredness of the Silk Cotton Tree. Among them is a young man named Ravi, whose greed and arrogance blinds him to the consequences of his actions. Determined to clear a patch of land for his own selfish purposes, Ravi sets his sights on a magnificent Silk Cotton Tree that stands in his way.

With axe in hand, Ravi approaches the Silk Cotton Tree, his heart filled with determination and his mind clouded by thoughts of riches and power. Ignoring the warnings of the villagers, he raises his axe high and strikes the tree with all his might, his actions echoing through the forest like a thunderclap.

But as the first blow falls, a sense of foreboding washes over Ravi, a feeling of unease that he cannot shake. Ignoring the warning signs, he continues to strike the tree, his axe biting deep into its ancient bark with each swing. And then, with a final blow, the tree comes crashing to the ground, its branches splintering and its leaves scattering like a flock of startled birds.

In the days that follow, strange things begin to happen to Ravi, his once-charmed life now plagued by misfortune and tragedy. Crops fail, livestock sicken, and loved ones fall ill, their bodies wasting away with a mysterious sickness that defies all attempts at a cure. And through it all, Ravi is haunted by the memory of the Silk Cotton Tree, its fallen branches a stark reminder of his folly.

Desperate to atone for his sins, Ravi seeks out the village elders, humbled by his experiences and seeking forgiveness for his actions. With tears in his eyes, he begs for their help, promising to do whatever it takes to make amends for his disrespect of the Silk Cotton Tree. And though the elders are wary of his sincerity, they see the remorse in his heart and agree to help him seek redemption.

Together, Ravi and the village elders embark on a journey to the site of the fallen Silk Cotton Tree, their hearts heavy with the weight of their task. With each step, they offer prayers and blessings to the spirits that dwell within the tree, seeking forgiveness for Ravi's transgressions and asking for the restoration of balance and harmony to the land.

And then, as they stand before the fallen tree, a miracle occurs. With a sudden burst of light, the branches of the Silk Cotton Tree begin to stir, their leaves rustling in the breeze as if awakened from a deep slumber. And then, to the amazement of all who witness it, the tree begins to grow anew, its branches reaching skyward once more as if to reclaim its rightful place in the world. As Ravi watches in awe, a sense of peace washes over him, his heart filled with gratitude for the opportunity to make amends for his past mistakes. And though the journey towards redemption may be long and difficult, he knows that with the guidance of the spirits and the support of his community, he will find his way back to the path of righteousness once more.

The Rhythms of Unity: The Legend of Bongo Man

In the vibrant tapestry of Trinidadian folklore, there exists a figure known as Bongo Man, a beloved icon celebrated for his extraordinary musical talents and infectious rhythm. Born amidst the pulsating heartbeat of the island, Bongo Man's legend is steeped in magic and mystery, his name whispered in reverence by those who have heard the enchanting melodies of his drum.

According to legend, Bongo Man was gifted with a magical drum that possessed the power to summon spirits and enchant listeners with its hypnotic beats. Crafted from the finest materials by the hands of the spirits themselves, this drum was imbued with the soul of Trinidad & Tobago, its rhythms reflecting the rich tapestry of cultures that called the island home.

From a young age, Bongo Man displayed an extraordinary talent for music, his fingers dancing across the drum's surface with a grace and precision that seemed otherworldly. With each beat, he conjured melodies that stirred the soul and ignited the spirit, his music weaving a tapestry of sound that transcended barriers of race, class, and creed.

As word of Bongo Man's talents spread throughout the island, people from all walks of life flocked to hear him play, drawn by the promise of an experience that transcended the ordinary. Wherever he went, crowds would gather to dance and celebrate, their bodies moving in perfect harmony to the hypnotic rhythms of his drums.

But it was not just Bongo Man's musical talents that captivated the hearts of the people. It was his spirit of unity and inclusivity, his belief that music had the power to bring people together in a harmonious celebration of life and culture. In his presence, barriers of race, class, and creed melted away, replaced by a sense of belonging and connection that touched the soul.

One night, as Bongo Man played beneath the stars, a stranger approached him with a gleam in his eye and a challenge on his lips. "I have heard of your extraordinary talents," the stranger said, his voice tinged with arrogance. "But I wonder if you truly possess the power to move the soul with your music."

Undaunted by the stranger's challenge, Bongo Man accepted, his fingers poised to unleash the full force of his musical magic. With a deep breath, he began to play, his drum resonating with a rhythm that seemed to echo the very heartbeat of the island itself. And as the music filled the air, a transformation occurred, as if the very fabric of reality had been woven anew.

With each beat of the drum, the stranger's skepticism melted away, replaced by a sense of wonder and awe that filled his heart to bursting. He danced and swayed to the rhythm, his movements mirroring the ebb and flow of the music as it surged through his veins like a tidal wave of emotion.

And then, as the last notes of Bongo Man's melody faded into the night, a sense of peace settled over the crowd, their hearts uplifted, and their spirits renewed by the power of his music. In that moment, they knew that they had witnessed something truly extraordinary, a testament to the magic of music and the soul of Trinidad & Tobago.

And so, the legend of Bongo Man lives on, a timeless tale of music and magic that continues to inspire and uplift all who hear it. For in his extraordinary talents and infectious rhythm, Bongo Man embodies the spirit of unity and inclusivity that lies at the heart of Trinidadian culture, reminding us all of the power of music to transcend barriers and bring people together in a harmonious celebration of life and culture.

Echoes of the Past: Unraveling the Mystery of Devil's Woodyard

In the heart of Trinidad lies a place shrouded in mystery and folklore, a natural geological formation known as Devil's Woodyard. Its name alone sends shivers down the spine, conjuring images of darkness and malevolence that have lingered for centuries. According to legend, Devil's Woodyard earned its ominous moniker from a group of devil worshippers who once inhabited the area, performing dark rituals and summoning evil spirits.

The origins of Devil's Woodyard's eerie reputation date back to a time long forgotten, when whispers of dark deeds and forbidden rituals echoed through the dense forests of Trinidad. It is said that a group of devil worshippers, driven by a thirst for power and forbidden knowledge, sought refuge in the secluded valley where Devil's Woodyard now stands. There, amidst the ancient trees and rugged landscape, they conducted their sinister rites, calling upon dark forces to grant them unimaginable power.

But as the devil worshippers delved deeper into their dark arts, their rituals grew increasingly twisted and depraved, their thirst for power consuming them like a ravenous flame. And it was not long before the malevolent energy they had unleashed began to manifest in terrifying ways, causing strange phenomena such as spontaneous fires and unexplained sounds that echoed through the night like the wails of tormented souls.

As word of the devil worshippers' dark deeds spread throughout the land, fear and superstition gripped the hearts of the villagers who lived nearby. They spoke in hushed tones of the cursed valley where Devil's Woodyard now stood, warning of the malevolent spirits that lurked within its depths, hungry for the souls of the living.

Despite its ominous reputation, Devil's Woodyard remained a place of intrigue and fascination, drawing visitors from far and wide who were intrigued by its supernatural history. They came in search of answers, eager to unravel the mysteries that lay hidden within its rugged terrain and ancient trees.

Among the curious souls drawn to Devil's Woodyard was a young archaeologist named Maya, whose fascination with Trinidad's folklore and legends had led her to embark on a journey of discovery. Armed with her knowledge and determination, Maya set out to uncover the truth behind Devil's Woodyard's eerie reputation, her heart filled with a sense of excitement and trepidation as she ventured into the heart of the cursed valley.

As Maya delved deeper into the mysteries of Devil's Woodyard, she found herself drawn into a world of darkness and despair, where the lines between reality and legend blurred and the echoes of the past reverberated through the air like a haunting melody. She uncovered ancient artifacts and mysterious symbols etched into the rocks, each one a clue to the sinister secrets that lay hidden within the valley's depths.

But as Maya's investigation progressed, she found herself plagued by strange phenomena that seemed to defy explanation. Spontaneous fires erupted from the ground without warning, their flames dancing in the night like the tongues of vengeful spirits. Unexplained sounds echoed through the valley, filling the air with a sense of unease that seemed to seep into Maya's very soul.

Undeterred by the dangers that surrounded her, Maya pressed on, her determination to uncover the truth outweighing her fear of the unknown. And then, one fateful night, as she stood beneath the shadow of Devil's Woodyard, she felt a presence stir within the darkness, a malevolent energy that seemed to reach out and envelop her in its icy embrace.

With a sense of dread creeping over her, Maya realized that she had stumbled upon something far more sinister than she had ever imagined. The devil worshippers' dark rituals had left a stain on the land that lingered long after their demise, a malevolent energy that pulsed through Devil's Woodyard like a heartbeat of darkness. And as Maya stood amidst the ancient trees and rugged terrain, she knew that she had uncovered a mystery that would haunt her dreams for years to come.

The Sanctum of Serenity: The Legend of Mount Saint Benedict

Nestled in the heart of the Northern Range of Trinidad, amidst the verdant beauty of the tropical rainforest, lies the majestic Mount Saint Benedict. Steeped in legend and spirituality, this sacred mountain is said to be home to a mystical monastery inhabited by monks who possess extraordinary powers of healing and enlightenment. According to folklore, pilgrims from far and wide journey to Mount Saint Benedict seeking solace and spiritual guidance, drawn by the promise of miraculous cures and divine interventions.

The origins of Mount Saint Benedict's mystical reputation date back centuries, to a time when Trinidad was a land of untamed wilderness and ancient spirits roamed the land. It is said that a group of monks, led by a visionary sage named Benedict, ventured into the heart of the Northern Range in search of a place where they could commune with the divine and dedicate their lives to prayer and contemplation.

After months of arduous journeying, the monks stumbled upon a secluded valley nestled amidst the rugged peaks of the Northern Range. There, amidst the towering trees and crystal-clear streams, they discovered a sense of serenity and tranquility unlike any they had ever known. And so, they decided to make this sacred valley their home, building a monastery atop Mount Saint Benedict that would serve as a beacon of light and hope for all who sought solace and spiritual guidance.

As word of the monastery's existence spread throughout the land, pilgrims from far and wide began to journey to Mount Saint Benedict, drawn by the promise of healing and enlightenment that awaited them amidst its hallowed grounds. They came in search of answers to life's deepest questions, seeking solace in the presence of the monks who dwelled within the monastery's walls.

Legend has it that the monks of Mount Saint Benedict possess extraordinary powers of healing and enlightenment, bestowed upon them by the divine. It is said that their prayers and blessings have the power to heal the sick and comfort the afflicted, their words carrying the weight of centuries of wisdom and spiritual guidance.

Among the pilgrims who journeyed to Mount Saint Benedict was a young woman named Maria, whose heart was heavy with grief and longing for solace. She had heard tales of the monastery's miraculous cures and divine interventions, and she hoped that the monks could help her find peace amidst the turmoil of her soul.

As Maria approached the monastery atop Mount Saint Benedict, she felt a sense of awe and reverence wash over her, the presence of the divine palpable in the air around her. With trembling hands, she knocked on the monastery's ancient wooden door, her heart pounding with anticipation as she awaited a response.

To Maria's surprise, the door swung open, revealing a serene courtyard bathed in the soft glow of twilight. Standing before her was a monk clad in simple robes, his eyes filled with compassion and understanding. Without a word, he gestured for Maria to follow him into the monastery, his silent presence offering comfort and reassurance in the face of her fears.

As Maria entered the monastery's hallowed halls, she felt a sense of peace wash over her, the weight of her grief lifting like a burden lifted from her shoulders. She spent days in prayer and contemplation, seeking solace in the presence of the monks who dwelled within the monastery's walls.

And then, one fateful night, as Maria knelt in prayer before the monastery's altar, she felt a presence stir within her soul, a sense of peace and clarity unlike any she had ever known. In that moment, she knew that she had found the solace and spiritual guidance she had been seeking, her heart forever changed by the sanctity of Mount Saint Benedict and the monks who dwelled within its hallowed grounds.

Printed in Great Britain
by Amazon